To Astrid Rose Allison

First published in hardback in Great Britain by Andersen Press Ltd in 2004
First published in paperback by HarperCollins Children's Books in 2006
This edition published in 2012

1 3 5 7 9 10 8 6 4 2

ISBN-13: 978-0-00-791279-7

HarperCollins Children's Books is a division of HarperCollins Publishers Ltd.

Text and illustrations copyright © Tony Ross 2004, 2006

Visit our website at: www.harpercollins.co.uk

Printed and bound by South China Printing Co.Ltd

I Want My Mum

Tony Ross

HarperCollins *Children's Books*

It was raining and the Little Princess was busy with her painting when the awful thing happened...

...she knocked her water pot over and she spoiled the best painting she had ever done.

"Don't worry," said the Maid, "everything's OK!"
And she mopped up the mess.
"I WANT MY MUM!" yelled the Little Princess.

Mum held up the soggy picture.
"That's WONDERFUL!" she said. "A rainy day."
The Little Princess smiled.

When the rain stopped, she went outside to play
on the see-saw and the terrible thing happened...
She banged her knee.

"There, there," said the Doctor. "That's OK now."
And she put some smelly stuff on it.
"I WANT MY MUM!" cried the Little Princess.

And Mum kissed the smelly knee better.
The Little Princess smiled.

That night, the Little Princess couldn't sleep
because of the monster living under the bed.

"There isn't a monster living under the bed,"
said Dad. "Look!" But the Little Princess daren't.
"I WANT MY MUM!" she screamed.

"I'll read stories to you and the monster," said Mum.

The Little Princess smiled. And fell asleep.

"I HATE eggs!" said the Little Princess at breakfast.

"Eat it up," said the Cook. "It's awfully good for you."

"I WANT MY MUM!" howled the Little Princess.

"Oh, GOODY!" said Mum. "Dinosaur eggs. I love those."
The Little Princess smiled. "Hey, save some for ME!"

All morning the Little Princess had to play by herself.
The Maid popped in to play Snakes and Ladders.
"I WANT MY MUM!" bawled the Little Princess.

The Admiral popped in to play boats.
"I WANT MY MUM!" hooted the Little Princess.

The Little Prince popped in to play anything at all.
And to stop the noise.
"I WANT MY MUM!" shrieked the Little Princess.

At last Mum came, with some thrilling news.
"The Little Duchess has asked you over for
a sleepover tonight, with crisps and a video."

The Little Princess packed her bag, and began to cry.
"What's the MATTER?" said Mum.

"I DON'T WANT TO GO!" sobbed the Little Princess.
"I WANT TO STAY HERE WITH GILBERT AND YOU!"
"But Gilbert and I are coming with you," said Mum.

At the Little Duchess's castle, the video
was turned on and Mum crept away.
"I WANT MY M..." began the Little Princess...

...but the video was terribly funny,
and the crisps were terribly good...

The Little Princess smiled.

Back at the Royal Palace,
the Queen was chatting to the King.
"She's having a wonderful time," she said. Then...

"I WANT MY LITTLE PRINCESS!"

Collect all the funny stories featuring the demanding Little Princess!

I Want My Potty — Tony Ross — 978-0-00-723621-3

I Want To Be — Tony Ross — 978-0-00-724282-5

I Want My Dinner — Tony Ross — 978-0-00-723620-6

I Want A Sister — Tony Ross — 978-0-00-724281-8

I Don't Want To Go To Hospital — Tony Ross — 978-0-00-710957-9

I Want My Dummy — 978-0-00-724283-2

I Don't Want To Wash My Hands — Tony Ross — 978-0-00-715072-4

I Want My Tooth — Tony Ross — 978-0-00-724365-5

I Don't Want To Go To Bed — Tony Ross — 978-0-00-725448-4

I Want My Mum — Tony Ross — 978-0-00-720033-7

I Want A Friend — Tony Ross — 978-0-00-721491-4

"The Little Princess has huge appeal to toddlers and Tony Ross's illustrations are brilliantly witty."
Practical Parenting

Tony Ross was born in London in 1938. His dream was to work with horses but instead he went to art college in Liverpool. Since then, Tony has worked as an art director at an advertising agency, a graphic designer, a cartoonist, a teacher and a film maker – as well as illustrating over 250 books!